JUL 21

To my sometimes similar and never the same children,
das A und O, Aaron and Olivia. —J.R.-Z.

All rights reserved. For information about permission to reproduce selections
from this book, write to trade.permissions@hmhco.com or to Permissions,
Houghton Mifflin Harcourt Publishing Company,
3 Park Avenue, 19th Floor, New York, New York 10016.

hmhbooks.com

The illustrations in this book were done in Procreate on an iPad.
The text was set in Clarendon LT Std.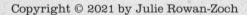
Interior design by Celeste Knudsen

Library of Congress Cataloging-in-Publication Data is on file.
ISBN 978-0-358-12506-8

Manufactured in China
SCP 10 9 8 7 6 5 4 3 2 1
4500815071

I'M A HARE, SO THERE!

By Julie Rowan-Zoch

Houghton Mifflin Harcourt
Boston   New York

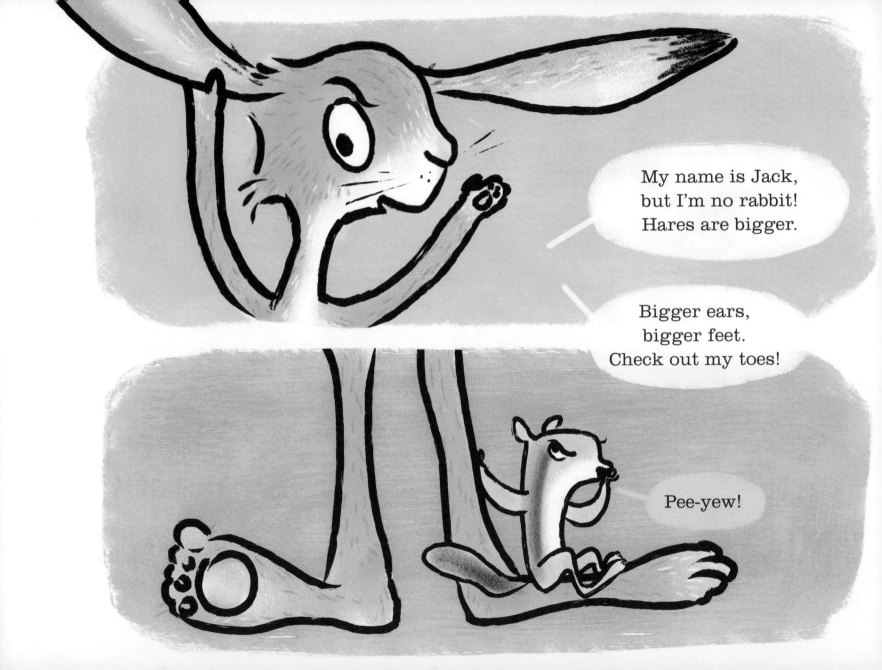

Like sheep and goats,
and they are NOT the same.

O-o-o-o-o

Frogs have moist, slimy skin.

Toads have dry, bumpy skin.

SIMILAR
but not the same

Lizards are reptiles and have scales.

Salamanders are amphibians and have moist skin.

Javelinas are smaller and have one dewclaw on each back leg.

Hogs are larger and have two!

Ravens are larger and make a low, croaking sound.

Crows are smaller and make a cawing sound.

Goats have hairy coats and their tails point up.

Sheep have wooly coats and their tails point down.

Tortoises live on land.

Turtles live in water some or nearly all of the time.

A hare's fur changes color in winter.

A rabbit's fur stays the same year-round.

Wasps have smooth bodies and thin waists.

Bees have hairy bodies and round bellies.